This edition first published in 2019 by Gecko Press
PO Box 9335, Wellington 6141, New Zealand
info@geckopress.com

English-language edition © Gecko Press Ltd 2019

Text and illustrations © Leo Timmers 2018
Originally published by Em. Querido's Uitgeverij, Amsterdam, the Netherlands
under the title *Aap op straat*
Translation rights arranged by élami agency

Typesetting by Katrina Duncan
Printed in China by Everbest Printing Co. Ltd, an accredited ISO 14001 & FSC certified printer

ISBN hardback: 978-1-776572-50-2
ISBN paperback: 978-1-776572-51-9

For more curiously good books, visit geckopress.com

MONKEY ON THE RUN

Leo Timmers

GECKO PRESS

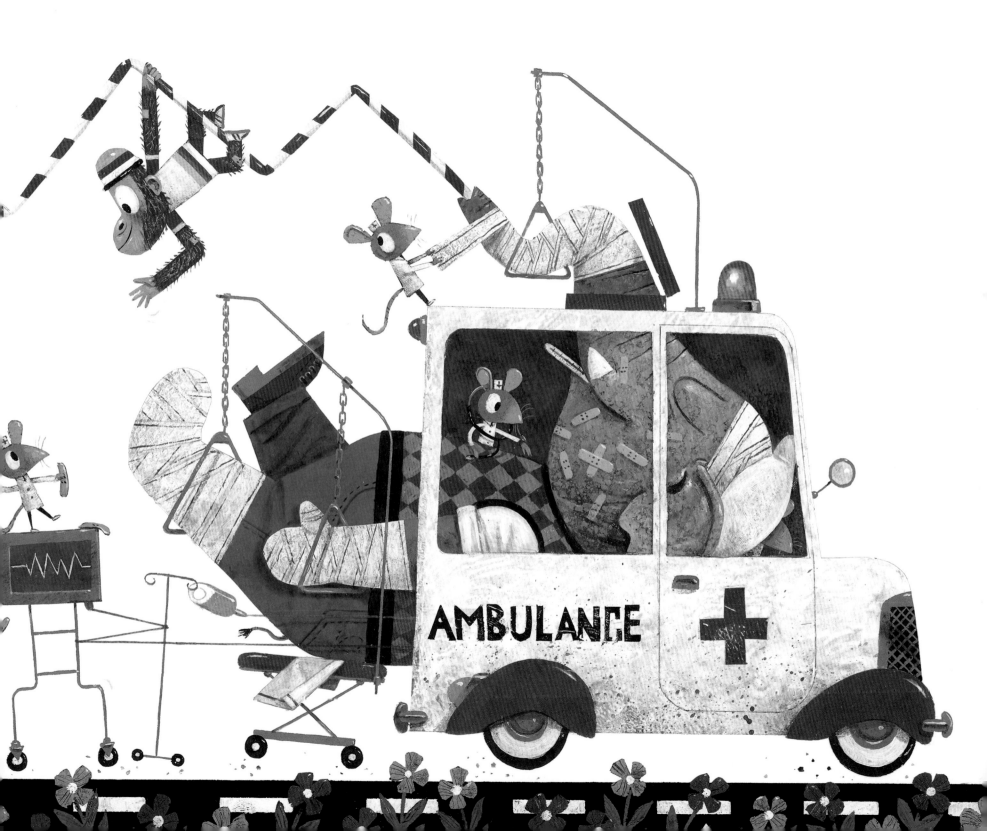

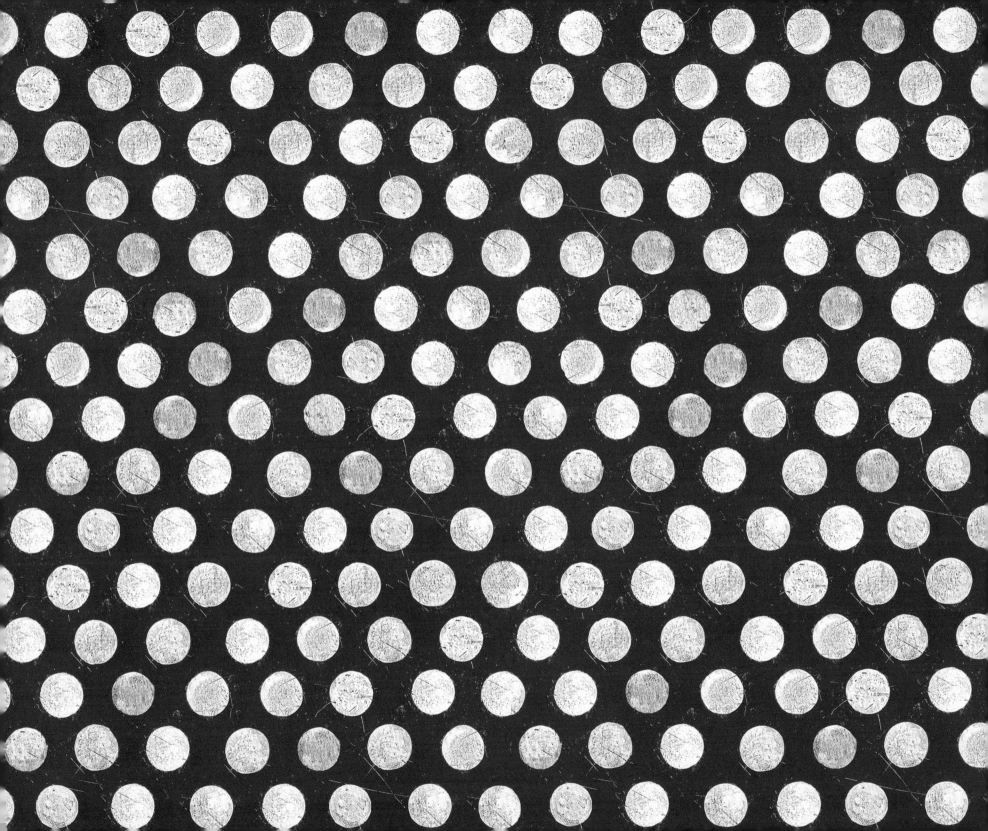

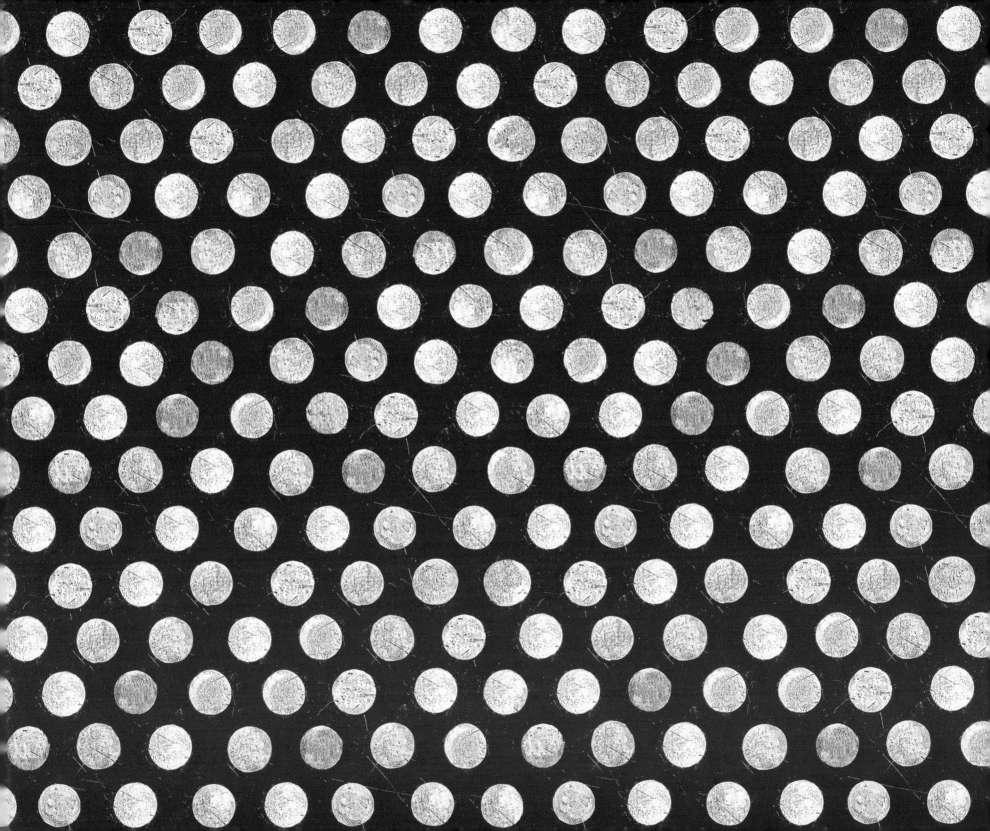